THE UNKNOWN MASTERPIECE

Honore De Balzac

Contents

THE UNKNOWN MASTERPIECE

BY

Honore De Balzac

I--GILLETTE

On a cold December morning in the year 1612, a young man, whose clothing was somewhat of the thinnest, was walking to and fro before a gateway in the Rue des Grands-Augustins in Paris. He went up and down the street before this house with the irresolution of a gallant who dares not venture into the presence of the mistress whom he loves for the first time, easy of access though she may be; but after a sufficiently long interval of hesitation, he at last crossed the threshold and inquired of an old woman, who was sweeping out a large room on the ground floor, whether Master Porbus was within. Receiving a reply in the affirmative, the young man went slowly up the staircase, like a gentleman but newly come to court, and doubtful as to his reception by the king. He came to a stand once more on the landing at the head of the stairs, and again he hesitated before raising his hand to the grotesque knocker on the door of the studio, where doubtless the painter was at work--Master Porbus, sometime painter in ordinary to Henri IV till Mary de' Medici took Rubens into favor.

The young man felt deeply stirred by an emotion that must thrill the hearts of all great artists when, in the pride of their youth and their first love of art, they come into the presence of a master or stand before a masterpiece. For all human sentiments there is a time of early blossoming, a day of generous enthusiasm that gradually fades until nothing is left of happiness but a memory, and glory is known for a delusion. Of all these delicate and short-lived emotions, none so resemble love as the passion of a young artist for his art, as he is about to enter on the blissful martyrdom of his career of glory and disaster, of vague expectations and real disappointments.

Those who have missed this experience in the early days of light purses; who have not, in the dawn of their genius, stood in the presence of a master and felt the throbbing of their hearts, will always carry in their inmost souls a chord that has never been touched, and in their work an indefinable quality will be lacking, a something in the stroke of the brush, a mysterious element that we call poetry. The swaggerers, so puffed up by self-conceit that they are confident over-soon of their success, can never be taken for men of talent save by fools. From this point of view, if youthful modesty is the measure of youthful genius, the stranger on the staircase might be allowed to have something in him; for he seemed to possess the indescribable diffidence, the early timidity that artists are bound to lose in the course of a great career, even as pretty women lose it as they make progress in the arts of coquetry. Self-distrust vanishes as triumph succeeds to triumph, and modesty is, perhaps, distrust of itself.

The poor neophyte was so overcome by the consciousness of his own presumption and insignificance, that it began to look as if he was hardly likely to penetrate into the studio of the painter, to whom we owe the wonderful portrait of Henri IV. But fate was propitious; an old man came up the staircase. From the quaint costume of this newcomer, his collar of magnificent lace, and a certain serene gravity in his bearing, the first arrival thought that this personage must be either a patron or a friend of the court painter. He stood aside therefore upon the landing to allow the visitor to pass, scrutinizing him curiously the while. Perhaps he might hope to find the good nature of an artist or to receive the good offices of an amateur not unfriendly to the arts; but besides an almost diabolical expression in the face that met his gaze, there was that indescribable something which has an irresistible attraction for artists.

Picture that face. A bald high forehead and rugged jutting brows above a small flat nose turned up at the end, as in the portraits of Socrates and Rabelais; deep lines about the mocking mouth; a short chin, carried proudly, covered with a grizzled pointed beard; sea-green eyes that age might seem to have dimmed were it not for the contrast between the iris and the surrounding mother-of-pearl tints, so that it seemed as if under the stress of anger or enthusiasm there would be a magnetic power to quell or kindle in their glances. The face was withered beyond wont by the fatigue of years, yet it seemed aged still more by the thoughts that had worn away both soul and body. There were no lashes to the deep-set eyes, and scarcely a trace of the arching lines of the eyebrows above them. Set this head on a spare and feeble frame, place it in a frame of lace wrought like an engraved silver fish-slice, imagine a heavy gold chain over the old man's black doublet, and you will have some dim idea of this strange personage, who seemed still more fantastic in the sombre twilight of the staircase. One of Rembrandt's portraits might have stepped down from its frame to walk in an appropriate atmosphere of gloom, such as the great painter loved. The older man gave the younger a shrewd glance, and knocked thrice at the door. It was opened by a man of forty or thereabout, who seemed to be an invalid.

"Good day, Master."

Porbus bowed respectfully, and held the door open for the younger man to enter, thinking that the latter accompanied his visitor; and when he saw that the neophyte stood a while as if spellbound, feeling, as every artist-nature must feel, the fascinating influence of the first sight of a studio in which the material processes of art are revealed, Porbus troubled himself no more about this second comer.

All the light in the studio came from a window in the roof, and was concentrated upon an easel, where a canvas stood untouched as yet save for three or four outlines in chalk. The daylight scarcely reached the remoter angles and corners of the vast room; they were as dark as night, but the silver ornamented breastplate of a Reiter's corselet, that hung upon the wall, attracted a stray gleam to its dim abiding-place among the brown shadows; or a shaft of light shot across the carved and glistening surface of an antique sideboard covered with curious silver-plate, or struck out a line of glittering dots among the raised threads of the golden warp of some old brocaded curtains, where the lines of the stiff, heavy folds were broken, as the stuff had been flung carelessly down to serve as a model.

Plaster *ecorches* stood about the room; and here and there, on shelves and tables, lay fragments of classical sculpture-torsos of antique goddesses, worn smooth as though all the years of the centuries that had passed over them had been lovers' kisses. The walls were covered, from floor to ceiling, with countless sketches in charcoal, red chalk, or pen and ink. Amid the litter and confusion of color boxes, overturned stools, flasks of oil, and essences, there was just room to move so as to reach the illuminated circular space where the easel stood. The light from the window in the roof fell full upon Por-bus's pale face and on the ivory-tinted forehead of his strange visitor. But in another moment the younger man heeded nothing but a picture that had already become famous even in those stormy days of political and religious revolution, a picture that a few of the zealous worshipers, who have so often kept the sacred fire of art alive in evil days, were wont to go on pilgrimage to see. The beautiful panel represented a Saint Mary of Egypt about to pay her passage across the seas. It was a masterpiece destined for Mary de' Medici, who sold it in later years of poverty.

"I like your saint," the old man remarked, addressing Porbus. "I would give you ten golden crowns for her over and above the price the Queen is paying; but as for putting a spoke in that wheel,--the devil take it!"

"It is good then?"

"Hey! hey!" said the old man; "good, say you?--Yes and no. Your good woman is not badly done, but she is not alive. You artists fancy that when a figure is correctly drawn, and everything in its place according to the rules of anatomy, there is nothing more to be done. You make up the flesh tints beforehand on your palettes according to your formulae, and fill in the outlines with due care that one side of the face shall be darker than the other; and because you look from time to time at a naked woman who stands on the platform before you, you fondly imagine that you have copied nature, think yourselves to be painters, believe that you have wrested His secret from God. Pshaw! You may know your syntax thoroughly and make no blunders in your grammar, but it takes that and something more to make a great poet. Look at your saint, Porbus! At a first glance she is admirable; look at her again, and you see at once that she is glued to the background, and that you could not walk round her. She is a silhouette that turns but one side of her face to all beholders, a figure cut out of canvas, an image with no power to move nor change her position. I feel as if there were no air between that arm and the background, no space, no sense of distance in your canvas. The perspective is perfectly correct, the strength of the coloring is accurately diminished with the distance; but, in spite of these praiseworthy efforts, I could never bring myself to believe that the warm breath of life comes and goes in that beautiful body. It seems to me that if I laid my hand on the firm, rounded throat, it would be cold as marble to the touch. No, my friend, the blood does not flow beneath that ivory skin, the tide of life does not flush those delicate fibres, the purple veins that trace a network beneath the transparent amber of her brow and breast. Here the pulse seems to beat, there it is motionless, life and death are at strife in every detail; here you see a woman, there a statue, there again a corpse. Your creation is incomplete. You had only power to breathe a portion of your soul into your beloved work. The fire of Prometheus died out again and again in your hands; many a spot in your picture has not been touched by the divine flame."

"But how is it, dear master?" Porbus asked respectfully, while the young man with difficulty repressed his strong desire to beat the critic.

"Ah!" said the old man, "it is this! You have halted between two manners. You have hesitated between drawing and color, between the dogged attention to detail, the stiff precision of the German masters and the dazzling glow, the joyous exuberance of Italian painters. You have set yourself to imitate Hans Holbein and Titian, Albrecht Durer and Paul Veronese in a single picture. A magnificent ambition truly, but what has come of it? Your work has neither the severe charm of a dry execution nor the magical illusion of Italian *chiaroscuro*. Titian's rich golden coloring poured into Albrecht Dureras austere outlines has shattered them, like molten bronze bursting through the mold that is not strong enough to hold it. In other places the outlines have held firm, imprisoning and obscuring the magnificent, glowing flood of Venetian color. The drawing of the face is not perfect, the coloring is not perfect; traces of that unlucky indecision are to be seen everywhere. Unless you felt strong enough to fuse the two opposed manners in the fire of your own genius, you should have cast in your lot boldly with the one or the other, and so have obtained the unity which simulates one of the conditions of life itself. Your work is only true in the centres; your outlines are false, they project nothing, there is no hint of anything behind them. There is truth here," said the old man, pointing to the breast of the Saint, "and again here," he went on, indicating the rounded shoulder. "But there," once more returning to the column of the throat, "everything is false. Let us go no further into detail, you would be disheartened."

The old man sat down on a stool, and remained a while without speaking, with his face buried in his hands.

"Yet I studied that throat from the life, dear master," Porbus began; "it happens sometimes, for our misfortune, that real effects in nature look improbable when transferred to canvas--"

"The aim of art is not to copy nature, but to express it. You are not a servile copyist, but a poet!" cried the old man sharply, cutting Porbus short with an imperious gesture. "Otherwise a sculptor might make a plaster cast of a living woman and save himself all further trouble. Well, try to make a cast of your mistress's hand, and set up the thing before you. You will see a monstrosity, a dead mass, bearing no resemblance to the living hand; you would be compelled to have recourse to the chisel of a sculptor who, without making an exact copy, would represent for you its movement and its life. We must detect the spirit, the informing soul in the appearances of things and beings. Effects! What are effects but the accidents of life, not life itself? A hand, since I have taken that example, is not only a part of a body, it is the expression and extension of a thought that must be grasped and rendered. Neither painter nor poet nor sculptor may separate the effect from the cause, which are inevitably contained the one in the other. There begins the real struggle! Many a painter achieves success instinctively, unconscious of the task that is set before art. You draw a woman, yet you do not see her! Not so do you succeed in wresting Nature's secrets from her! You are reproducing mechanically the model that you copied in your master's studio. You do not penetrate far enough into the inmost secrets of the mystery of form; you do not seek with love enough and perseverance enough after the form that baffles and eludes you. Beauty is a thing severe and unapproachable, never to be won by a languid lover. You must lie in wait for her coming and take her unawares, press her hard and clasp her in a tight embrace, and force her to yield. Form is a Proteus more intangible and more manifold than the Proteus of the legend; compelled, only after long wrestling, to stand forth manifest in his true aspect. Some of you are satisfied with the first shape, or at most by the second or the third that appears. Not thus wrestle the victors, the unvanquished painters who never suffer themselves to be deluded by all those treacherous shadow-shapes; they persevere till Nature at the last stands bare to their gaze, and her very soul is revealed.

"In this manner worked Rafael," said the old man, taking off his cap to express his reverence for the King of Art. "His transcendent greatness came of the intimate sense that, in him, seems as if it would shatter external form. Form in his figures (as with us) is a symbol, a means of communicating sensations, ideas, the vast imaginings of a poet. Every face is a whole world. The subject of the portrait appeared for him bathed in the light of a divine vision; it was revealed by an inner voice, the finger of God laid bare the sources of expression in the past of a whole life.

"You clothe your women in fair raiment of flesh, in gracious veiling of hair; but where is the blood, the source of passion and of calm, the cause of the particular effect? Why, this brown Egyptian of yours, my good Porbus, is a colorless creature! These figures that you set before us are painted bloodless fantoms; and you call that painting, you call that art!

"Because you have made something more like a woman than a house, you think that you have set your fingers on the goal; you are quite proud that you need not to write *currus venustus* or *pulcher homo* beside your figures, as early painters were wont to do and you fancy that you have done wonders. Ah! my good friend, there is still something more to learn, and you will use up a great deal of chalk and cover many a canvas before you will learn it. Yes, truly, a woman carries her head in just such a way, so she holds her garments gathered into her hand; her eyes grow dreamy and soft with that expression of meek sweetness, and even so the quivering shadow of the lashes hovers upon her cheeks. It is all there, and yet it is not there. What is lacking? A nothing, but that nothing is everything.

"There you have the semblance of life, but you do not express its fulness and effluence, that indescribable something, perhaps the soul itself, that envelopes the outlines of the body like a haze; that flower of life, in short, that Titian and Rafael caught. Your utmost achievement hitherto has only brought you to the starting-point. You might now perhaps begin to do excellent work, but you grow weary all too soon; and the crowd admires, and those who know smile.

"Oh, Mabuse! oh, my master!" cried the strange speaker, "thou art a thief! Thou hast carried away the secret of life with thee!"

"Nevertheless," he began again, "this picture of yours is worth more than all the paintings of that rascal Rubens, with his mountains of Flemish flesh raddled with vermilion, his torrents of red hair, his riot of color. You, at least have color there, and feeling and drawing--the three essentials in art."

The young man roused himself from his deep musings.

"Why, my good man, the Saint is sublime!" he cried.

"There is a subtlety of imagination about those two figures, the Saint Mary and the Shipman, that can not be found among Italian masters; I do not know a single one of them capable of imagining the Shipman's hesitation."

"Did that little malapert come with you?" asked Porbus of the older man.

"Alas! master, pardon my boldness," cried the neophyte, and the color mounted to his face. "I am unknown--a dauber by instinct, and but lately come to this city--the fountain-head of all learning."

"Set to work," said Porbus, handing him a bit of red chalk and a sheet of paper.

The new-comer quickly sketched the Saint Mary line for line.

"Aha!" exclaimed the old man. "Your name?" he added.

The young man wrote "Nicolas Poussin" below the sketch.

"Not bad that for a beginning," said the strange speaker, who had discoursed so wildly. "I see that we can talk of art in your presence. I do not blame you for admiring

Porbus's saint. In the eyes of the world she is a masterpiece, and those alone who have been initiated into the inmost mysteries of art can discover her shortcomings. But it is worth while to give you the lesson, for you are able to understand it, so I will show you how little it needs to complete this picture. You must be all eyes, all attention, for it may be that such a chance of learning will never come in your way again--Porbus! your palette."

Porbus went in search of palette and brushes. The little old man turned back his sleeves with impatient energy, seized the palette, covered with many hues, that Porbus handed to him, and snatched rather than took a handful of brushes of various sizes from the hands of his acquaintance. His pointed beard suddenly bristled--a menacing movement that expressed the prick of a lover's fancy. As he loaded his brush, he muttered between his teeth, "These paints are only fit to fling out of the window, together with the fellow who ground them, their crudeness and falseness are disgusting! How can one paint with this?"

He dipped the tip of the brush with feverish eagerness in the different pigments, making the circuit of the palette several times more quickly than the organist of a cathedral sweeps the octaves on the keyboard of his clavier for the "O Filii" at Easter.

Porbus and Poussin, on either side of the easel, stood stock-still, watching with intense interest.

"Look, young man," he began again, "see how three or four strokes of the brush and a thin glaze of blue let in the free air to play about the head of the poor Saint, who must have felt stifled and oppressed by the close atmosphere! See how the drapery begins to flutter; you feel that it is lifted by the breeze! A moment ago it hung as heavily and stiffly as if it were held out by pins. Do you see how the satin sheen that I have just given to the breast rends the pliant, silken softness of a young girl's skin, and how the brown-red, blended with burnt ochre, brings warmth into the cold gray of the deep shadow where the blood lay congealed instead of coursing through the veins? Young man, young man, no master could teach you how to do this that I am doing before your eyes. Mabuse alone possessed the secret of giving life to his figures; Mabuse had but one pupil--that was I. I have had none, and I am old. You have sufficient intelligence to imagine the rest from the glimpses that I am giving you."

While the old man was speaking, he gave a touch here and there; sometimes two strokes of the brush, sometimes a single one; but every stroke told so well, that the whole picture seemed transfigured--the painting was flooded with light. He worked with such passionate fervor that beads of sweat gathered upon his bare forehead; he worked so quickly, in brief, impatient jerks, that it seemed to young Poussin as if some familiar spirit inhabiting the body of this strange being took a grotesque pleasure in making use of the man's hands against his own will. The unearthly glitter of his eyes, the convulsive movements that seemed like struggles, gave to this fancy a semblance of truth which could not but stir a young imagination. The old man continued, saying as he did so--

"Paf! paf! that is how to lay it on, young man!--Little touches! come and bring a glow into those icy cold tones for me! Just so! Pon! pon! pon!" and those parts of the picture that he had pointed out as cold and lifeless flushed with warmer hues, a few bold strokes of color brought all the tones of the picture into the required harmony with the glowing tints of the Egyptian, and the differences in temperament vanished.

"Look you, youngster, the last touches make the picture. Porbus has given it a hundred strokes for every one of mine. No one thanks us for what lies beneath. Bear that in mind."

At last the restless spirit stopped, and turning to Porbus and Poussin, who were speechless with admiration, he spoke--

"This is not as good as my 'Belle Noiseuse'; still one might put one's name to such a thing as this.--Yes, I would put my name to it," he added, rising to reach for a mirror, in which he looked at the picture.--"And now," he said, "will you both come and breakfast with me? I have a smoked ham and some very fair wine!... Eh! eh! the times may be bad, but we can still have some talk about art! We can talk like equals.... Here is a little fellow who has aptitude," he added, laying a hand on Nicolas Poussin's shoulder.

In this way the stranger became aware of the threadbare condition of the Norman's doublet. He drew a leather purse from his girdle, felt in it, found two gold coins, and held them out.

"I will buy your sketch," he said.

"Take it," said Porbus, as he saw the other start and flush with embarrassment, for Poussin had the pride of poverty. "Pray, take it; he has a couple of king's ransoms in his pouch!"

The three came down together from the studio, and, talking of art by the way, reached a picturesque wooden house hard by the Pont Saint-Michel. Poussin wondered a moment at its ornament, at the knocker, at the frames of the casements, at the scroll-work designs, and in the next he stood in a vast low-ceiled room. A table, covered with tempting dishes, stood near the blazing fire, and (luck unhoped for) he was in the company of two great artists full of genial good humor.

"Do not look too long at that canvas, young man," said Porbus, when he saw that Poussin was standing, struck with wonder, before a painting. "You would fall a victim to despair."

It was the "Adam" painted by Mabuse to purchase his

release from the prison, where his creditors had so long kept him. And, as a matter of fact, the figure stood out so boldly and convincingly, that Nicolas Poussin began to understand the real meaning of the words poured out by the old artist, who was himself looking at the picture with apparent satisfaction, but without enthusiasm. "I have done better than that!" he seemed to be saying to himself.

"There is life in it," he said aloud; "in that respect my poor master here surpassed himself, but there is some lack of truth in the background. The man lives indeed; he is rising, and will come toward us; but the atmosphere, the sky, the air, the breath of the breeze--you look and feel for them, but they are not there. And then the man himself is, after all, only a man! Ah! but the one man in the world who came direct from the hands of God must have had a something divine about him that is wanting here. Mabuse himself would grind his teeth and say so when he was not drunk."

Poussin looked from the speaker to Porbus, and from Porbus to the speaker, with restless curiosity. He went up to the latter to ask for the name of their host; but the painter laid a finger on his lips with an air of mystery. The young man's interest was excited; he kept silence, but hoped that sooner or later some word might be let fall that would reveal the name of his entertainer. It was evident that he was a man of talent and very wealthy, for Porbus listened to him respectfully, and the vast room was crowded with marvels of art.

A magnificent portrait of a woman, hung against the dark oak panels of the wall, next caught Poussin's attention.

"What a glorious Giorgione!" he cried.

"No," said his host, "it is an early daub of mine--"

"Gramercy! I am in the abode of the god of painting, it seems!" cried Poussin ingenuously.

The old man smiled as if he had long grown familiar with such praise.

"Master Frenhofer!" said Porbus, "do you think you could spare me a little of your capital Rhine wine?"

"A couple of pipes!" answered his host; "one to discharge a debt, for the pleasure of seeing your pretty sinner, the other as a present from a friend."

"Ah! if I had my health," returned Porbus, "and if

you would but let me see your 'Belle Noiseuse,' I would paint some great picture, with breadth in it and depth; the figures should be life-size."

"Let you see my work!" cried the painter in agitation. "No, no! it is not perfect yet; something still remains for me to do. Yesterday, in the dusk," he said, "I thought I had reached the end. Her eyes seemed moist, the flesh quivered, something stirred the tresses of her hair. She breathed! But though I have succeeded in reproducing Nature's roundness and relief on the flat surface of the canvas, this morning, by daylight, I found out my mistake. Ah! to achieve that glorious result I have studied the works of the great masters of color, stripping off coat after coat of color from Titian's canvas, analyzing the pigments of the king of light. Like that sovereign painter, I began the face in a slight tone with a supple and fat paste--for shadow is but an accident; bear that in mind, youngster!--Then I began afresh, and by half-tones and thin glazes of color less and less transparent, I gradually deepened the tints to the deepest black of the strongest shadows. An ordinary painter makes his shadows something entirely different in nature from the high lights; they are wood or brass, or what you will, anything but flesh in shadow. You feel that even if those figures were to alter their position, those shadow stains would never be cleansed away, those parts of the picture would never glow with light.

"I have escaped one mistake, into which the most famous painters have sometimes fallen; in my canvas the whiteness shines through the densest and most persistent shadow. I have not marked out the limits of my figure in hard, dry outlines, and brought every least anatomical detail into prominence (like a host of dunces, who fancy that they can draw because they can trace a line elaborately smooth and clean), for the human body is not contained within the limits of line. In this the sculptor can approach the truth more nearly than we painters. Nature's way is a complicated succession of curve within curve. Strictly speaking, there is no such thing as drawing.--Do not laugh, young man; strange as that speech may seem to you, you will understand the truth in it some day.--A line is a method of expressing the effect of light upon an object; but there are no lines in Nature, everything is solid. We draw by modeling, that is to say, that we disengage an object from its setting; the distribution of the light alone gives to a body the appearance by which we know it. So I have not defined the outlines; I have suffused them with a haze of half-tints warm or golden, in such a sort that you can not lay your finger on the exact spot where background and contours meet. Seen from near, the picture looks a blur; it seems to lack definition; but step back two paces, and the whole thing becomes clear, distinct, and solid; the body stands out; the rounded form comes into relief; you feel that the air plays round it. And yet--I am not satisfied; I have misgivings. Perhaps one ought not to draw a single line; perhaps it would be better to attack the face from the centre, taking the highest prominences first, proceeding from them through the whole range of shadows to the heaviest of all. Is not this the method of the sun, the divine painter of the world? Oh, Nature, Nature! who has surprised thee, fugitive? But, after all, too much knowledge, like ignorance, brings you to a negation. I have doubts about my work."

There was a pause. Then the old man spoke again. "I have been at work upon it for ten years, young man;

but what are ten short years in a struggle with Nature? Do we know how long Sir Pygmalion wrought at the one statue that came to life?" The old man fell into deep musings, and gazed before him with unseeing eyes, while he played unheedingly with his knife.

"Look, he is in conversation with his *domon!*" murmured Porbus.

At the word, Nicolas Poussin felt himself carried away by an unaccountable accession of artist's curiosity. For him the old man, at once intent and inert, the seer with the unseeing eyes, became something more than a man--a fantastic spirit living in a mysterious world, and countless vague thoughts awoke within his soul. The effect of this species of fascination upon his mind can no more be described in words than the passionate longing awakened in an exile's heart by the song that recalls his home. He thought of the scorn that the old man affected to display for the noblest efforts of art, of his wealth, his manners, of the deference paid to him by Porbus. The mysterious picture, the work of patience on which he had wrought so long in secret, was doubtless a work of genius, for the head of the Virgin which young Poussin had admired so frankly was beautiful even beside Mabuse's "Adam"--there was no mistaking the imperial manner of one of the princes of art. Everything combined to set the old man beyond the limits of human nature.

Out of the wealth of fancies in Nicolas Poussin's brain an idea grew, and gathered shape and clearness. He saw in this supernatural being a complete type of the artist nature, a nature mocking and kindly, barren and prolific, an erratic spirit intrusted with great and manifold powers which she too often abuses, leading sober reason, the Philistine, and sometimes even the amateur forth into a stony wilderness where they see nothing; but the white-winged maiden herself, wild as her fancies may be, finds epics there and castles and works of art. For Poussin, the enthusiast, the old man, was suddenly transfigured, and became Art incarnate, Art with its mysteries, its vehement passion and its dreams.

"Yes, my dear Porbus," Frenhofer continued, "hitherto I have never found a flawless model, a body with outlines of perfect beauty, the carnations--Ah! where does she live?" he cried, breaking in upon himself, "the undiscoverable Venus of the older time, for whom we have sought so often, only to find the scattered gleams of her beauty here and there? Oh! to behold once and for one moment, Nature grown perfect and divine, the Ideal at last, I would give all that I possess.... Nay, Beauty divine, I would go to seek thee in the dim land of the dead; like Orpheus, I would go down into the Hades of Art to bring back the life of art from among the shadows of death."

"We can go now," said Porbus to Poussin. "He neither hears nor sees us any longer."

"Let us go to his studio," said young Poussin, wondering greatly.

"Oh! the old fox takes care that no one shall enter it. His treasures are so carefully guarded that it is impossible for us to come at them. I have not waited for your suggestion and your fancy to attempt to lay hands on this mystery by force."

"So there is a mystery?" "Yes," answered Porbus. "Old Frenhofer is the only pupil Mabuse would take. Frenhofer became the painter's friend, deliverer, and father; he sacrificed the greater part of his fortune to enable Mabuse to indulge in riotous extravagance, and in return Mabuse bequeathed to him the secret of relief, the power of giving to his figures the wonderful life, the flower of Nature, the eternal despair of art, the secret which Ma-buse knew so well that one day when he had sold the flowered brocade suit in which he should have appeared at the Entry of Charles V, he accompanied his master in a suit of paper painted to resemble the brocade. The peculiar richness and splendor of the stuff struck the Emperor; he complimented the old drunkard's patron on the artist's appearance, and so the trick was brought to light. Frenhofer is a passionate enthusiast, who sees above and beyond other painters. He has meditated profoundly on color, and the absolute truth of line; but by the way of much research he has come to doubt the very existence of the objects of his search. He says, in moments of despondency, that there is no such thing as drawing, and that by means of lines we can only reproduce geometrical figures; but that is overshooting the mark, for by outline and shadow you can reproduce form without any color at all, which shows that our art, like Nature, is composed of an infinite number of elements. Drawing gives you the skeleton, the anatomical frame-' work, and color puts the life into it; but life without the skeleton is even more incomplete than a skeleton without life. But there is something else truer still, and it is this--f or painters, practise and observation are everything; and when theories and poetical ideas begin to quarrel with the brushes, the end is doubt, as has happened with our good friend, who is half crack-brained enthusiast, half painter. A sublime painter! but unlucky for him, he was born to riches, and so he has leisure to follow his fancies. Do not you follow his example! Work! painters have no business to think, except brush in hand."

"We will find a way into his studio!" cried Poussin confidently. He had ceased to heed Porbus's remarks. The other smiled at the young painter's enthusiasm, asked him to come to see him again, and they parted. Nicolas Poussin went slowly back to the Rue de la Harpe, and passed the modest hostelry where he was lodging without noticing it. A feeling of uneasiness prompted him to hurry up the crazy staircase till he reached a room at the top, a quaint, airy recess under the steep, high-pitched roof common among houses in old Paris. In the one dingy window of the place sat a young girl, who sprang up at once when she heard some one at the door; it was the prompting of love; she had recognized the painter's touch on the latch.

"What is the matter with you?" she asked.

"The matter is... is... Oh! I have felt that I am a painter! Until to-day I have had doubts, but now I believe in myself! There is the making of a great man in me! Never mind, Gillette, we shall be rich and happy! There is gold at the tips of those brushes--"

He broke off suddenly. The joy faded from his powerful and earnest face as he compared his vast hopes with his slender resources. The walls were covered with sketches in chalk on sheets of common paper. There were but four canvases in the room. Colors were very costly, and the young painter's palette was almost bare. Yet in the midst of his poverty he possessed and was conscious of the possession of inexhaustible treasures of the heart, of a devouring genius equal to all the tasks that lay before him.

He had been brought to Paris by a nobleman among

his friends, or perchance by the consciousness of his powers; and in Paris he had found a mistress, one of those noble and generous souls who choose to suffer by a great man's side, who share his struggles and strive to understand his fancies, accepting their lot of poverty and love as bravely and dauntlessly as other women will set themselves to bear the burden of riches and make a parade of their insensibility. The smile that stole over Gillette's lips filled the garret with golden light, and rivaled the brightness of the sun in heaven. The sun, moreover, does not always shine in heaven, whereas Gillette was always in the garret, absorbed in her passion, occupied by Poussin's happiness and sorrow, consoling the genius which found an outlet in love before art engrossed it.

"Listen, Gillette. Come here."

The girl obeyed joyously, and sprang upon the painter's knee. Hers was perfect grace and beauty, and the loveliness of spring; she was adorned with all luxuriant fairness of outward form, lighted up by the glow of a fair soul within.

"Oh! God," he cried; "I shall never dare to tell her--"

"A secret?" she cried; "I must know it!"

Poussin was absorbed in his dreams.

"Do tell it me!"

"Gillette... poor beloved heart!..."

"Oh! do you want something of me?"

"Yes."

"If you wish me to sit once more for you as I did the other day," she continued with playful petulance, "I will never consent to do such a thing again, for your eyes say nothing all the while. You do not think of me at all, and yet you look at me--"

"Would you rather have me draw another woman?"

"Perhaps--if she were very ugly," she said.

"Well," said Poussin gravely, "and if, for the sake of my fame to come, if to make me a great painter, you must sit to some one else?"

"You may try me," she said; "you know quite well that I would not."

Poussin's head sank on her breast; he seemed to be overpowered by some intolerable joy or sorrow.

"Listen," she cried, plucking at the sleeve of Poussin's threadbare doublet, "I told you, Nick, that I would lay down my life for you; but I never promised you that I in my lifetime would lay down my love."

"Your love?" cried the young artist.

"If I showed myself thus to another, you would love me no longer, and I should feel myself unworthy of you. Obedience to your fancies was a natural and simple thing, was it not? Even against my own will, I am glad and even proud to do thy dear will. But for another, out upon it!"

"Forgive me, my Gillette," said the painter, falling upon his knees; "I would rather be beloved than famous. You are fairer than success and honors. There, fling the pencils away, and burn these sketches! I have made a mistake. I was meant to love and not to paint. Perish art and all its secrets!"

Gillette looked admiringly at him, in an ecstasy of happiness! She was triumphant; she felt instinctively that art was laid aside for her sake, and flung like a grain of incense at her feet.

"Yet he is only an old man," Poussin continued; "for him you would be a woman, and nothing more. You-- so perfect!"

"I must love you indeed!" she cried, ready to sacrifice even love's scruples to the lover who had given up so much for her sake; "but I should bring about my own ruin. Ah! to ruin myself, to lose everything for you!... It is a very glorious thought! Ah! but you will forget me. Oh I what evil thought is this that has come to you?"

"I love you, and yet I thought of it," he said, with something like remorse, "Am I so base a wretch?"

"Let us consult Pere Hardouin," she said.

"No, no! Let it be a secret between us."

"Very well; I will do it. But you must not be there," she said. "Stay at the door with your dagger in your hand; and if I call, rush in and kill the painter."

Poussin forgot everything but art. He held Gillette tightly in his arms.

"He loves me no longer!" thought Gillette when she was alone. She repented of her resolution already.

But to these misgivings there soon succeeded a sharper pain, and she strove to banish a hideous thought that arose in her own heart. It seemed to her that her own love had grown less already, with a vague suspicion that the painter had fallen somewhat in her eyes.

II--CATHERINE LESCAULT

Three months after Poussin and Porbus met, the latter went to see Master Frenhofer. The old man had fallen a victim to one of those profound and spontaneous fits of discouragement that are caused, according to medical logicians, by indigestion, flatulence, fever, or enlargement of the spleen; or, if you take the opinion of the Spiritualists, by the imperfections of our mortal nature. The good man had simply overworked himself in putting the finishing touches to his mysterious picture. He was lounging in a huge carved oak chair, covered with black leather, and did not change his listless attitude, but glanced at Porbus like a man who has settled down into low spirits.

"Well, master," said Porbus, "was the ultramarine bad that you sent for to Bruges? Is the new white difficult to grind? Is the oil poor, or are the brushes recalcitrant?"

"Alas!" cried the old man, "for a moment I thought that my work was finished, but I am sure that I am mistaken in certain details, and I can not rest until I have cleared my doubts. I am thinking of traveling. I am going to Turkey, to Greece, to Asia, in quest of a model, so as to compare my picture with the different living forms of Nature. Perhaps," and a smile of contentment stole over his face, "perhaps I have Nature herself up there. At times I am half afraid that a breath may waken her, and that she will escape me."

He rose to his feet as if to set out at once.

"Aha!" said Porbus, "I have come just in time to save you the trouble and expense of a journey."

"What?" asked Frenhofer in amazement.

"Young Poussin is loved by a woman of incomparable and flawless beauty. But, dear master, if he consents to lend her to you, at the least you ought to let us see your work."

The old man stood motionless and completely dazed.

"What!" he cried piteously at last, "show you my creation, my bride? Rend the veil that has kept my happiness sacred? It would be an infamous profanation. For ten years I have lived with her; she is mine, mine alone; she loves me. Has she not smiled at me, at each stroke of the brush upon the canvas? She has a soul--the soul that I have given her. She would blush if any eyes but mine should rest on her. To exhibit her! Where is the husband, the lover so vile as to bring the woman he loves to dishonor? When you paint a picture for the court, you do not put your whole soul into it; to courtiers you sell lay figures duly colored. My painting is no painting, it is a sentiment, a passion. She was born in my studio, there she must dwell in maiden solitude, and only when clad can she issue thence. Poetry and women only lay the last veil aside for their lovers Have we Rafael's model, Ariosto's Angelica, Dante's Beatrice? Nay, only their form and semblance. But this picture, locked away above in my studio, is an exception in our art. It is not a canvas, it is a woman--a woman with whom I talk. I share her thoughts, her tears, her laughter. Would you have me fling aside these ten years of happiness like a cloak? Would you have me cease at once to be father, lover, and creator? She is not a creature, but a creation.

"Bring your young painter here. I will give him my treasures; I will give him pictures by Correggio and Michelangelo and Titian; I will kiss his footprints in the dust; but make him my rival! Shame on me. Ah! ah! I am a lover first, and then a painter. Yes, with my latest sigh I could find strength to burn my 'Belle Noiseuse'; but--compel her to endure the gaze of a stranger, a young man and a painter!--Ah! no, no! I would kill him on the morrow who should sully her with a glance! Nay, you, my friend, I would kill you with my own hands in a moment if you did not kneel in reverence before her! Now, will you have me submit my idol to the careless eyes and senseless criticisms of fools? Ah! love is a mystery; it can only live hidden in the depths of the heart. You say, even to your friend, 'Behold her whom I love,' and there is an end of love."

The old man seemed to have grown young again; there was light and life in his eyes, and a faint flush of red in his pale face. His hands shook. Porbus was so amazed by the passionate vehemence of Frenhofer's words that he knew not what to reply to this utterance of an emotion as strange as it was profound. Was Frenhofer sane or mad? Had he fallen a victim to some freak of the artist's fancy? or were these ideas of his produced by the strange lightheadedness which comes over us during the long travail of a work of art. Would it be possible to come to terms with this singular passion?

Harassed by all these doubts, Porbus spoke--"Is it not woman for woman?" he said. "Does not Poussin submit his mistress to your gaze?"

"What is she?" retorted the other. "A mistress who will be false to him sooner or later. Mine will be faithful to me forever."

"Well, well," said Porbus, "let us say no more about it. But you may die before you will find such a flawless beauty as hers, even in Asia, and then your picture will be left unfinished.

"Oh! it is finished," said Frenhof er. "Standing before it you would think that it was a living woman lying on the velvet couch beneath the shadow of the curtains. Perfumes are burning on a golden tripod by her side. You would be tempted to lay your hand upon the tassel of the cord that holds back the curtains; it would seem to you that you saw her breast rise and fall as she breathed; that you beheld the living Catherine Lescault, the beautiful courtezan whom men called 'La Belle Noiseuse.' And yet--if I could but be sure--"

"Then go to Asia," returned Porbus, noticing a certain indecision in Frenhofer's face. And with that Porbus made a few steps toward the door. By that time Gillette and Nicolas Poussin had reached Frenhofer's house. The girl drew away her arm from her lover's as she stood on the threshold, and shrank back as if some presentiment flashed through her mind.

"Oh! what have I come to do here?" she asked of her lover in low vibrating tones, with her eyes fixed on his.

"Gillette, I have left you to decide; I am ready to obey you in everything. You are my conscience and my glory. Go home again; I shall be happier, perhaps, if you do not--"

"Am I my own when you speak to me like that? No, no; I am a child.--Come," she added, seemingly with a violent effort; "if our love dies, if I plant a long regret in my heart, your fame will be the reward of my obedience to your wishes, will it not? Let us go in. I shall still live on as a memory on your palette; that shall be life for me afterward."

The door opened, and the two lovers encountered Porbus, who was surprised by the beauty of Gillette, whose eyes were full of tears. He hurried her, trembling from head to foot, into the presence of the old painter.

"Here!" he cried, "is she not worth all the masterpieces in the world!"

Frenhofer trembled. There stood Gillette in the artless and childlike attitude of some timid and innocent Georgian, carried off by brigands, and confronted with a slave merchant. A shamefaced red flushed her face, her eyes drooped, her hands hung by her side, her strength seemed to have failed her, her tears protested against this outrage. Poussin cursed himself in despair that he should have brought his fair treasure from its hiding-place. The lover overcame the artist, and countless doubts assailed Poussin's heart when he saw youth dawn in the old man's eyes, as, like a painter, he discerned every line of the form hidden beneath the young girl's vesture. Then the lover's savage jealousy awoke.

"Gillette!" he cried, "let us go."

The girl turned joyously at the cry and the tone in which it was uttered, raised her eyes to his, looked at him, and fled to his arms.

"Ah! then you love me," she cried; "you love me!" and she burst into tears.

She had spirit enough to suffer in silence, but she had no strength to hide her joy.

"Oh! leave her with me for one moment," said the old painter, "and you shall compare her with my Catherine... yes--I consent."

Frenhofer's words likewise came from him like a lover's cry. His vanity seemed to be engaged for his semblance of womanhood; he anticipated the triumph of the beauty of his own creation over the beauty of the living girl.

"Do not give him time to change his mind!" cried Porbus, striking Poussin on the shoulder. "The flower of love soon fades, but the flower of art is immortal."

"Then am I only a woman now for him?" said Gillette. She was watching Poussin and Porbus closely.

She raised her head proudly; she glanced at Frenhofer, and her eyes flashed; then as she saw how her lover had fallen again to gazing at the portrait which he had taken at first for a Giorgione--

"Ah!" she cried; "let us go up to the studio. He never gave me such a look."

The sound of her voice recalled Poussin from his dreams.

"Old man," he said, "do you see this blade? I will plunge it into your heart at the first cry from this young girl; I will set fire to your house, and no one shall leave it alive. Do you understand?"

Nicolas Poussin scowled; every word was a menace. Gillette took comfort from the young painter's bearing, and yet more from that gesture, and almost forgave him for sacrificing her to his art and his glorious future.

Porbus and Poussin stood at the door of the studio and looked at each other in silence. At first the painter of the Saint Mary of Egypt hazarded some exclamations: "Ah! she has taken off her clothes; he told her to come into the light--he is comparing the two!" but the sight of the deep distress in Poussin's face suddenly silenced him; and though old painters no longer feel these scruples, so petty in the presence of art, he admired them because they were so natural and gracious in the lover. The young man kept his hand on the hilt of his dagger, and his ear was almost glued to the door. The two men standing in the shadow might have been conspirators waiting for the hour when they might strike down a tyrant.

"Come in, come in," cried the old man. He was radiant with delight. "My work is perfect. I can show her now with pride. Never shall painter, brushes, colors, light, and canvas produce a rival for 'Catherine Lescault,' the beautiful courtezan!"

Porbus and Poussin, burning with eager curiosity, hurried into a vast studio. Everything was in disorder and covered with dust, but they saw a few pictures here and there upon the wall. They stopped first of all in admiration before the life-size figure of a woman partially draped.

"Oh! never mind that," said Frenhofer; "that is a rough daub that I made, a study, a pose, it is nothing. These are my failures," he went on, indicating the enchanting compositions upon the walls of the studio.

This scorn for such works of art struck Porbus and

Poussin dumb with amazement. They looked round for the picture of which he had spoken, and could not discover it.

"Look here!" said the old man. His hair was disordered, his face aglow with a more than human exaltation, his eyes glittered, he breathed hard like a young lover frenzied by love.

"Aha!" he cried, "you did not expect to see such perfection! You are looking for a picture, and you see a woman before you. There is such depth in that canvas, the atmosphere is so true that you can not distinguish it from the air that surrounds us. Where is art? Art has vanished, it is invisible! It is the form of a living girl that you see before you. Have I not caught the very hues of life, the spirit of the living line that defines the figure? Is there not the effect produced there like that which all natural objects present in the atmosphere about them, or fishes in the water? Do you see how the figure stands out against the background? Does it not seem to you that you pass your hand along the back? But then for seven years I studied and watched how the daylight blends with the objects on which it falls. And the hair, the light pours over it like a flood, does it not?... Ah! she breathed, I am sure that she breathed! Her breast--ah, see! Who would not fall on his knees before her? Her pulses throb. She will rise to her feet. Wait!"

"Do you see anything?" Poussin asked of Porbus.

"No... do you?"

"I see nothing."

The two painters left the old man to his ecstasy, and tried to ascertain whether the light that fell full upon the canvas had in some way neutralized all the effect for them. They moved to the right and left of the picture; they came in front, bending down and standing upright by turns.

"Yes, yes, it is really canvas," said Frenhofer, who mistook the nature of this minute investigation.

"Look! the canvas is on a stretcher, here is the easel; indeed, here are my colors, my brushes," and he took up a brush and held it out to them, all unsuspicious of their thought.

"The old *lansquenet* is laughing at us," said Poussin, coming once more toward the supposed picture. "I can see nothing there but confused masses of color and a multitude of fantastical lines that go to make a dead wall of paint."

"We are mistaken, look!" said Porbus.

In a corner of the canvas, as they came nearer, they distinguished a bare foot emerging from the chaos of color, half-tints and vague shadows that made up a dim, formless fog. Its living delicate beauty held them spell-bound. This fragment that had escaped an incomprehensible, slow, and gradual destruction seemed to them like the Parian marble torso of some Venus emerging from the ashes of a ruined town.

"There is a woman beneath," exclaimed Porbus, calling Poussin's attention to the coats of paint with which the old artist had overlaid and concealed his work in the quest of perfection.

Both artists turned involuntarily to Frenhofer. They began to have some understanding, vague though it was, of the ecstasy in which he lived.

"He believes it in all good faith," said Porbus.

"Yes, my friend," said the old man, rousing himself from his dreams, "it needs faith, faith in art, and you must live for long with your work to produce such a creation. What toil some of those shadows have cost me. Look! there is a faint shadow there upon the cheek beneath the eyes--if you saw that on a human face, it would seem to you that you could never render it with paint. Do you think that that effect has not cost unheard of toil?

"But not only so, dear Porbus. Look closely at my work, and you will understand more clearly what I was saying as to methods of modeling and outline. Look at the high lights on the bosom, and see how by touch on touch, thickly laid on, I have raised the surface so that it catches the light itself and blends it with the lustrous whiteness of the high lights, and how by an opposite process, by flattening the surface of the paint, and leaving no trace of the passage of the brush, I have succeeded in softening the contours of my figures and enveloping them in half-tints until the very idea of drawing, of the means by which the effect is produced, fades away, and the picture has the roundness and relief of nature. Come closer. You will see the manner of working better; at a little distance it can not be seen. There I Just there, it is, I think, very plainly to be seen," and with the tip of his brush he pointed out a patch of transparent color to the two painters.

Porbus, laying a hand on the old artist's shoulder, turned to Poussin with a "Do you know that in him we see a very great painter?"

"He is even more of a poet than a painter," Poussin answered gravely.

"There," Porbus continued, as he touched the canvas, "Use the utmost limit of our art on earth."

"Beyond that point it loses itself in the skies," said Poussin.

"What joys lie there on this piece of canvas!" exclaimed Porbus.

The old man, deep in his own musings, smiled at the woman he alone beheld, and did not hear.

"But sooner or later he will find out that there is nothing there!" cried Poussin.

"Nothing on my canvas!" said Frenhofer, looking in turn at either painter and at his picture.

"What have you done?" muttered Porbus, turning to Poussin.

The old man clutched the young painter's arm and

said, "Do you see nothing? clodpatel Huguenot! varlet! cullion! What brought you here into my studio?--My good Porbus," he went on, as he turned to the painter, "are you also making a fool of me? Answer! I am your friend. Tell me, have I ruined my picture after all?"

Porbus hesitated and said nothing, but there was such intolerable anxiety in the old man's white face that he pointed to the easel.

"Look!" he said.

Frenhofer looked for a moment at his picture, and staggered back.

"Nothing! nothing! After ten years of work..." He sat down and wept.

"So I am a dotard, a madman, I have neither talent nor power! I am only a rich man, who works for his own pleasure, and makes no progress, I have done nothing after all!"

He looked through his tears at his picture. Suddenly he rose and stood proudly before the two painters.

"By the body and blood of Christ," he cried with flashing eyes, "you are jealous! You would have me think that my picture is a failure because you want to steal her from me! Ah! I see her, I see her," he cried "she is marvelously beautiful..."

At that moment Poussin heard the sound of weeping; Gillette was crouching forgotten in a corner. All at once the painter once more became the lover. "What is it, my angel?" he asked her.

"Kill me!" she sobbed. "I must be a vile thing if I love you still, for I despise you.... I admire you, and I hate you! I love you, and I feel that I hate you even now!"

While Gillette's words sounded in Poussin's ears, Frenhof er drew a green serge covering over his "Catherine" with the sober deliberation of a jeweler who locks his drawers when he suspects his visitors to be expert thieves. He gave the two painters a profoundly astute glance that expressed to the full his suspicions, and his contempt for them, saw them out of his studio with impetuous haste and in silence, until from the threshold of his house he bade them "Good-by, my young friends!"

That farewell struck a chill of dread into the two painters. Porbus, in anxiety, went again on the morrow to see Frenhofer, and learned that he had died in the night after burning his canvases. Paris, February, 1832.

The Codes Of Hammurabi And Moses
W. W. Davies

QTY

The discovery of the Hammurabi Code is one of the greatest achievements of archaeology, and is of paramount interest, not only to the student of the Bible, but also to all those interested in ancient history...

Religion   **ISBN:** *1-59462-338-4*   **Pages:132**
MSRP $12.95

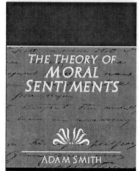

The Theory of Moral Sentiments
Adam Smith

QTY

This work from 1749. contains original theories of conscience amd moral judgment and it is the foundation for systemof morals.

Philosophy **ISBN:** *1-59462-777-0*   **Pages:536**
MSRP $19.95

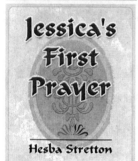

Jessica's First Prayer
Hesba Stretton

QTY

In a screened and secluded corner of one of the many railway-bridges which span the streets of London there could be seen a few years ago, from five o'clock every morning until half past eight, a tidily set-out coffee-stall, consisting of a trestle and board, upon which stood two large tin cans, with a small fire of charcoal burning under each so as to keep the coffee boiling during the early hours of the morning when the work-people were thronging into the city on their way to their daily toil...

Pages:84

Childrens   **ISBN:** *1-59462-373-2*   *MSRP $9.95*

My Life and Work
Henry Ford

QTY

Henry Ford revolutionized the world with his implementation of mass production for the Model T automobile. Gain valuable business insight into his life and work with his own auto-biography... "We have only started on our development of our country we have not as yet, with all our talk of wonderful progress, done more than scratch the surface. The progress has been wonderful enough but..."

Pages:300

Biographies/   **ISBN:** *1-59462-198-5*   *MSRP $21.95*

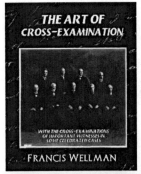

The Art of Cross-Examination
Francis Wellman

I presume it is the experience of every author, after his first book is published upon an important subject, to be almost overwhelmed with a wealth of ideas and illustrations which could readily have been included in his book, and which to his own mind, at least, seem to make a second edition inevitable. Such certainly was the case with me; and when the first edition had reached its sixth impression in five months, I rejoiced to learn that it seemed to my publishers that the book had met with a sufficiently favorable reception to justify a second and considerably enlarged edition. ..

QTY

Pages:412

Reference   **ISBN: *1-59462-647-2***   *MSRP $19.95*

On the Duty of Civil Disobedience
Henry David Thoreau

Thoreau wrote his famous essay, On the Duty of Civil Disobedience, as a protest against an unjust but popular war and the immoral but popular institution of slave-owning. He did more than write—he declined to pay his taxes, and was hauled off to gaol in consequence. Who can say how much this refusal of his hastened the end of the war and of slavery ?

QTY

Pages:48

Law   **ISBN: *1-59462-747-9***   *MSRP $7.45*

Dream Psychology Psychoanalysis for Beginners
Sigmund Freud

Sigmund Freud, born Sigismund Schlomo Freud (May 6, 1856 - September 23, 1939), was a Jewish-Austrian neurologist and psychiatrist who co-founded the psychoanalytic school of psychology. Freud is best known for his theories of the unconscious mind, especially involving the mechanism of repression; his redefinition of sexual desire as mobile and directed towards a wide variety of objects; and his therapeutic techniques, especially his understanding of transference in the therapeutic relationship and the presumed value of dreams as sources of insight into unconscious desires.

QTY

Pages:196

Psychology   **ISBN: *1-59462-905-6***   *MSRP $15.45*

The Miracle of Right Thought
Orison Swett Marden

Believe with all of your heart that you will do what you were made to do. When the mind has once formed the habit of holding cheerful, happy, prosperous pictures, it will not be easy to form the opposite habit. It does not matter how improbable or how far away this realization may see, or how dark the prospects may be, if we visualize them as best we can, as vividly as possible, hold tenaciously to them and vigorously struggle to attain them, they will gradually become actualized, realized in the life. But a desire, a longing without endeavor, a yearning abandoned or held indifferently will vanish without realization.

QTY

Pages:360

Self Help   **ISBN: *1-59462-644-8***   *MSRP $25.45*

QTY

The Rosicrucian Cosmo-Conception Mystic Christianity *by Max Heindel*   ISBN: *1-59462-188-8*   **$38.95**
The Rosicrucian Cosmo-conception is not dogmatic, neither does it appeal to any other authority than the reason of the student. It is: not controversial, but is: sent forth in the, hope that it may help to clear...   New Age/Religion Pages 646

Abandonment To Divine Providence *by Jean-Pierre de Caussade*   ISBN: *1-59462-228-0*   **$25.95**
"The Rev. Jean Pierre de Caussade was one of the most remarkable spiritual writers of the Society of Jesus in France in the 18th Century. His death took place at Toulouse in 1751. His works have gone through many editions and have been republished...   Inspirational Religion Pages 400

Mental Chemistry *by Charles Haanel*   ISBN: *1-59462-192-6*   **$23.95**
Mental Chemistry allows the change of material conditions by combining and appropriately utilizing the power of the mind. Much like applied chemistry creates something new and unique out of careful combinations of chemicals the mastery of mental chemistry...   New Age Pages 354

The Letters of Robert Browning and Elizabeth Barret Barrett 1845-1846 vol II   ISBN: *1-59462-193-4*   **$35.95**
by Robert Browning and Elizabeth Barrett
Biographies Pages 596

Gleanings In Genesis (volume I) *by Arthur W. Pink*   ISBN: *1-59462-130-6*   **$27.45**
Appropriately has Genesis been termed "the seed plot of the Bible" for in it we have, in germ form, almost all of the great doctrines which are afterwards fully developed in the books of Scripture which follow...   Religion Inspirational Pages 420

The Master Key *by L. W. de Laurence*   ISBN: *1-59462-001-6*   **$30.95**
In no branch of human knowledge has there been a more lively increase of the spirit of research during the past few years than in the study of Psychology, Concentration and Mental Discipline. The requests for authentic lessons in Thought Control, Mental Discipline and...   New Age Business Pages 422

The Lesser Key Of Solomon Goetia *by L. W. de Laurence*   ISBN: *1-59462-092-X*   **$9.95**
This translation of the first book of the "Lernegton" which is now for the first time made accessible to students of Talismanic Magic was done, after careful collation and edition, from numerous Ancient Manuscripts in Hebrew, Latin, and French...   New Age/Occult Pages 92

Rubaiyat Of Omar Khayyam *by Edward Fitzgerald*   ISBN: *1-59462-332-5*   **$13.95**
Edward Fitzgerald, whom the world has already learned, in spite of his own efforts to remain within the shadow of anonymity, to look upon as one of the rarest poets of the century, was born at Bredfield, in Suffolk, on the 31st of March, 1809. He was the third son of John Purcell...   Music Pages 172

Ancient Law *by Henry Maine*   ISBN: *1-59462-128-4*   **$29.95**
The chief object of the following pages is to indicate some of the earliest ideas of mankind, as they are reflected in Ancient Law, and to point out the relation of those ideas to modern thought.   Religiom History Pages 452

Far-Away Stories *by William J. Locke*   ISBN: *1-59462-129-2*   **$19.45**
"Good wine needs no bush, but a collection of mixed vintages does. And this book is just such a collection. Some of the stories I do not want to remain buried for ever in the museum files of dead magazine-numbers an author's not unpardonable vanity..."   Fiction Pages 272

Life of David Crockett *by David Crockett*   ISBN: *1-59462-250-7*   **$27.45**
"Colonel David Crockett was one of the most remarkable men of the times in which he lived. Born in humble life, but gifted with a strong will, an indomitable courage, and unremitting perseverance...   Biographies New Age Pages 424

Lip-Reading *by Edward Nitchie*   ISBN: *1-59462-206-X*   **$25.95**
Edward B. Nitchie, founder of the New York School for the Hard of Hearing, now the Nitchie School of Lip-Reading, Inc, wrote "LIP-READING Principles and Practice". The development and perfecting of this meritorious work on lip-reading was an undertaking...   How-to Pages 400

A Handbook of Suggestive Therapeutics, Applied Hypnotism, Psychic Science   ISBN: *1-59462-214-0*   **$24.95**
by Henry Munro
Health/New Age/Health Self-help Pages 376

A Doll's House: and Two Other Plays *by Henrik Ibsen*   ISBN: *1-59462-112-8*   **$19.95**
Henrik Ibsen created this classic when in revolutionary 1848 Rome. Introducing some striking concepts in playwriting for the realist genre, this play has been studied the world over.   Fiction Classics Plays 308

The Light of Asia *by sir Edwin Arnold*   ISBN: *1-59462-204-3*   **$13.95**
In this poetic masterpiece, Edwin Arnold describes the life and teachings of Buddha. The man who was to become known as Buddha to the world was born as Prince Gautama of India but he rejected the worldly riches and abandoned the reigns of power when...   Religion/History/Biographies Pages 170

The Complete Works of Guy de Maupassant *by Guy de Maupassant*   ISBN: *1-59462-157-8*   **$16.95**
"For days and days, nights and nights, I had dreamed of that first kiss which was to consecrate our engagement, and I knew not on what spot I should put my lips..."   Fiction Classics Pages 240

The Art of Cross-Examination *by Francis L. Wellman*   ISBN: *1-59462-309-0*   **$26.95**
Written by a renowned trial lawyer, Wellman imparts his experience and uses case studies to explain how to use psychology to extract desired information through questioning.   How-to Science/Reference Pages 408

Answered or Unanswered? *by Louisa Vaughan*   ISBN: *1-59462-248-5*   **$10.95**
Miracles of Faith in China
Religion Pages 112

The Edinburgh Lectures on Mental Science (1909) *by Thomas*   ISBN: *1-59462-008-3*   **$11.95**
This book contains the substance of a course of lectures recently given by the writer in the Queen Street Hall, Edinburgh. Its purpose is to indicate the Natural Principles governing the relation between Mental Action and Material Conditions...   New Age/Psychology Pages 148

Ayesha *by H. Rider Haggard*   ISBN: *1-59462-301-5*   **$24.95**
Verily and indeed it is the unexpected that happens! Probably if there was one person upon the earth from whom the Editor of this, and of a certain previous history, did not expect to hear again...   Classics Pages 380

Ayala's Angel *by Anthony Trollope*   ISBN: *1-59462-352-X*   **$29.95**
The two girls were both pretty, but Lucy who was twenty-one who supposed to be simple and comparatively unattractive, whereas Ayala was credited, as her Bombwhat romantic name might show, with poetic charm and a taste for romance. Ayala when her father died was nineteen...   Fiction Pages 484

The American Commonwealth *by James Bryce*   ISBN: *1-59462-286-8*   **$34.45**
An interpretation of American democratic political theory. It examines political mechanics and society from the perspective of Scotsman James Bryce   Politics Pages 572

Stories of the Pilgrims *by Margaret P. Pumphrey*   ISBN: *1-59462-116-0*   **$17.95**
This book explores pilgrims religious oppression in England as well as their escape to Holland and eventual crossing to America on the Mayflower, and their early days in New England...   History Pages 268

QTY

The Fasting Cure *by Sinclair Upton*   ISBN: *1-59462-222-1* **$13.95**
In the Cosmopolitan Magazine for May, 1910, and in the Contemporary Review (London) for April, 1910, I published an article dealing with my experiences in fasting. I have written a great many magazine articles, but never one which attracted so much attention... New Age/Self Help/Health Pages 164

Hebrew Astrology *by Sepharial*   ISBN: *1-59462-308-2* **$13.45**
In these days of advanced thinking it is a matter of common observation that we have left many of the old landmarks behind and that we are now pressing forward to greater heights and to a wider horizon than that which represented the mind-content of our progenitors... Astrology Pages 144

Thought Vibration or The Law of Attraction in the Thought World   ISBN: *1-59462-127-6* **$12.95**
by William Walker Atkinson   *Psychology/Religion Pages 144*

Optimism *by Helen Keller*   ISBN: *1-59462-108-X* **$15.95**
Helen Keller was blind, deaf, and mute since 19 months old, yet famously learned how to overcome these handicaps, communicate with the world, and spread her lectures promoting optimism. An inspiring read for everyone... Biographies/Inspirational Pages 84

Sara Crewe *by Frances Burnett*   ISBN: *1-59462-360-0* **$9.45**
In the first place, Miss Minchin lived in London. Her home was a large, dull, tall one, in a large, dull square, where all the houses were alike, and all the sparrows were alike, and where all the door-knockers made the same heavy sound... Childrens/Classic Pages 88

The Autobiography of Benjamin Franklin *by Benjamin Franklin*   ISBN: *1-59462-135-7* **$24.95**
The Autobiography of Benjamin Franklin has probably been more extensively read than any other American historical work, and no other book of its kind has had such ups and downs of fortune. Franklin lived for many years in England, where he was agent... Biographies/History Pages 332

Name	
Email	
Telephone	
Address	
City, State ZIP	

☐ **Credit Card**   ☐ **Check / Money Order**

Credit Card Number	
Expiration Date	
Signature	

Please Mail to: Book Jungle
PO Box 2226
Champaign, IL 61825
or Fax to: 630-214-0564

ORDERING INFORMATION

web*: www.bookjungle.com*
email*: sales@bookjungle.com*
fax*: 630-214-0564*
mail*: Book Jungle PO Box 2226 Champaign, IL 61825*
or PayPal *to sales@bookjungle.com*

Please contact us for bulk discounts

DIRECT-ORDER TERMS

**20% Discount if You Order
Two or More Books**
Free Domestic Shipping!
Accepted: Master Card, Visa,
Discover, American Express

CPSIA information can be obtained at www.ICGtesting.com
Printed in the USA
BVOW06s0621100114

341431BV00005B/86/P